THIS NOTEBOOK BELONG TO

NAME:

PHONE:

EMAIL:

NOTE:

Made in the USA
Monee, IL
27 April 2022

95528413R00069